THIS BOOK
BELONGS TO:

OTHER BOOKS WRITTEN BY **KATE KLISE**
AND ILLUSTRATED BY **M. SARAH KLISE**

THREE-RING RASCALS
THE GREATEST STAR ON EARTH

43 OLD CEMETERY ROAD
DYING TO MEET YOU
OVER MY DEAD BODY
TILL DEATH DO US BARK
THE PHANTOM OF THE POST OFFICE
HOLLYWOOD, DEAD AHEAD
GREETINGS FROM THE GRAVEYARD

REGARDING THE FOUNTAIN
REGARDING THE SINK
REGARDING THE TREES
REGARDING THE BATHROOMS
REGARDING THE BEES

LETTERS FROM CAMP
TRIAL BY JOURNAL

SHALL I KNIT YOU A HAT?
WHY DO YOU CRY?
IMAGINE HARRY
LITTLE RABBIT AND THE NIGHT MARE
LITTLE RABBIT AND THE MEANEST MOTHER ON EARTH
STAND STRAIGHT, ELLA KATE
GRAMMY LAMBY AND THE SECRET HANDSHAKE

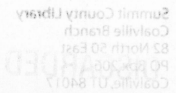

BOOK 1
Three-Ring
Rascals

THE
SHOW
MUST GO ON!

KATE KLISE

ILLUSTRATED BY
M. SARAH KLISE

ALGONQUIN YOUNG READERS • 2014

Published by
Algonquin Young Readers
An imprint of Algonquin Books of Chapel Hill
P.O. Box 2225, Chapel Hill, NC 27514

a division of
Workman Publishing
225 Varick Street, New York, New York 10014

Text © 2013 by Kate Klise. Illustrations © 2013 by M. Sarah Klise.
All rights reserved.
First paperback edition, Algonquin Young Readers, April 2014.
Originally published in hardcover by Algonquin Young Readers in 2013.
Printed in the United States of America.
Published simultaneously in Canada by Thomas Allen & Son Limited.
Design by M. Sarah Klise.

This is a work of fiction. While, as in all fiction, the literary perceptions
and insights are based on experience, all names, characters, places, and incidents
either are products of the author's imagination or are used fictitiously.

LIBRARY OF CONGRESS CATALOGING-IN-PUBLICATION DATA
Klise, Kate.
The show must go on! / Kate Klise ; illustrated by M. Sarah Klise.
pages cm—(Three-ring rascals ; book 1)
Summary: Two mice and a crow, who travel with a circus,
cleaning up the spilled popcorn after every performance, come to the rescue
when a greedy con artist takes over the management of the circus.
ISBN 978-1-61620-244-6 (HC)
[1. Circus—Fiction.]   I. Klise, M. Sarah, illustrator.   II. Title.
PZ7.K684Sj 2013
[Fic]—dc23   2013008940

ISBN 978-1-61620-406-8 (PB)

10 9 8 7 6 5 4 3 2 1
First Paperback Edition

This book is dedicated to **MILO**,
who wanted a funny book
about a mean baddie.

BOOK 1
Three-Ring Rascals

THE
SHOW
MUST GO ON!

If you're ever walking down a dusty road and see a sign that looks like this, **STOP** and look closely.

Then, look around and see if you can find an old man named Sir Sidney. He's the owner of Sir Sidney's Circus, which happens to be the **BEST** circus in the whole wide world.

Sir Sidney is a prince of a man. No one treats animals better than Sir Sidney does.

He grooms Leo the lion daily, with only the finest Italian brushes.

He has fresh peanuts flown in from his private peanut farm in Georgia. These are for Elsa the elephant.

He even built bunk beds for the Famous Flying Banana Brothers.

For years, Sir Sidney and his circus traveled to towns and cities around the world. Were audiences always amazed?

Were they dazzled and delighted?

Did people gasp and giggle and wave and wiggle?

Were children admitted **FREE OF CHARGE** and given all the hot popcorn they could possibly eat?

"And did we clean up after every show by eating all the spilled popcorn?"

You bet!

I'm Bert.

I'm Gert.

Aw! Aw!

And that's Old Coal the crow.

But during all those years of travel, did Sir Sidney grow old and tired? He most certainly did. He needed someone to help him.

So not long ago, Sir Sidney placed an ad in the newspaper.

Well, you can imagine the response! Hundreds of men and women stood in line for hours for a chance to talk to Sir Sidney.

Sir Sidney noticed that many people who wanted the job showed more respect for him than for his performers.

Others were afraid of the animals.

Still others were just, well, *wrong*.

But Sir Sidney met a man at the very end of the line who claimed to be PERFECT for the job.

He handed Sir Sidney a business card.

"I see," said Sir Sidney. "But Leo the lion is old, like me, and already quite tame."

That guy needs a job.

And a new suit. I hate to see a man in a bad suit.

"Tame, yes," agreed Barnabas Brambles. "But a bit dull, too. You're not exactly a barrel of laughs, either, if you don't mind my saying so."

"Oh dear," replied Sir Sidney. "Maybe you're right."

"I *know* I'm right!" said Barnabas Brambles. "What your circus needs is energy! Vision! A new attitude!"

"Maybe you have a point," Sir Sidney said.

"I see only a whip," Bert said to Gert.

"I have a point *and* a whip!" Barnabas Brambles bragged. "Hire me, Sir Sidney. I'm the best candidate for the job. You won't be disappointed!"

Sir Sidney spent the next day thinking about all the people who wanted the job. He made notes and lists.

He crossed off some names and circled others.

He also paced.

Finally, when Sir Sidney had made his decision, he wrote a letter and asked Old Coal to deliver it.

SIR SIDNEY'S CIRCUS

Sir Sidney
Owner and Founder

September 1

Barnabas Brambles
Certified Lion Tamer
1150 W. Fullerton Avenue
Chicago, IL 60614

Dear Mr. Brambles,

I hereby hire you to manage my circus for one week. You will make all the decisions and have complete responsibility. In return, you will receive the profits from all performances next week.

The only thing I ask is that you treat the members of my circus, both large and small, with the respect they deserve.

I will spend the week resting at my private peanut farm in Georgia. But I promise to attend one show so that I can see my dear friends and enjoy the new energy I know you will bring to my circus.

Please report to work immediately.

Sincerely,

Sir Sidney

Sir Sidney

P.S. Good luck!

Well... Barnabas Brambles wasted no time. First, he displayed his diploma for everyone to see and admire.

OFFICIAL DIPLOMA

UNIVERSITY of PICCADILLY CIRCUS
London, England

BARNABAS B. BRAMBLES

CERTIFIED LION TAMER

Authorized to tame, train, and boss around
lions, tigers, cougars, panthers,
and any other creatures, large or small,
that need taming, training, or bossing around
today, tomorrow, and forever.

Macon Upaname
Macon Upaname
Dean of Students

Then he studied the schedule.

This Week's Performances

Peoria (Monday)

Tulsa (Wednesday)

Denver (Friday)

San Francisco (Sunday)

Note: For the sake of our performers,
Sir Sidney's Circus presents
only one show
in every city we visit.

Tickets are $1 per adult.
Children are admitted free of charge.

Popcorn and lemonade are free.

"Only four shows in a week?" Barnabas Brambles said, rubbing his chin. "Why that's just . . . "

He pulled out a pad of paper and calculated the profits.

$$250 \text{ seats}$$
$$\times \ 4 \text{ shows}$$
$$\overline{}$$
$$1,000 \text{ customers}$$

$$1,000 \text{ customers}$$
$$\times \ \$1 \text{ ticket price}$$
$$\overline{}$$
$$\$1,000$$

"One thousand dollars," he said. "But half the people who come to the circus will be kids who get in for free." He grunted as he subtracted half of one thousand dollars.

$$\$1,000 \div 2 = \$500$$

$$\$1,000$$
$$- \ \$500$$
$$\overline{}$$
$$\$500 \text{ profit}$$

"That's no good," Barnabas Brambles grumbled. So he made a few quick changes to the schedule with his pen.

This Week's Performances

Peoria (Monday)
ST. LOUIS (TUESDAY)
Tulsa (Wednesday)
OKLAHOMA CITY (THURSDAY)
Denver (Friday)
LAS VEGAS (SATURDAY)
San Francisco (Sunday)

Note: For the sake of our ~~performers~~, BUSINESS

Sir Sidney's Circus presents

~~only one~~ THREE show**s**

in every city we visit.

Tickets are ~~$1~~ $5 per adult.

Children are admitted ~~free of charge.~~
FOR THE SAME PRICE AS ADULTS.

Popcorn and lemonade are ~~free~~ EXPENSIVE.

Barnabas Brambles recalculated the profits. "Let's see," he said.

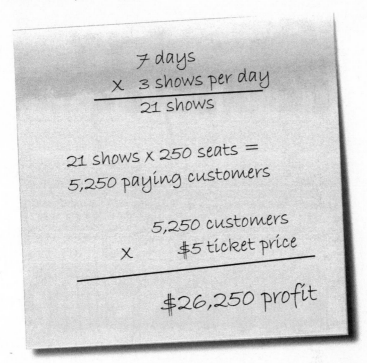

$$7 \text{ days}$$
$$\times \quad 3 \text{ shows per day}$$
$$\overline{21 \text{ shows}}$$

$$21 \text{ shows} \times 250 \text{ seats} =$$
$$5{,}250 \text{ paying customers}$$

$$5{,}250 \text{ customers}$$
$$\times \quad \$5 \text{ ticket price}$$
$$\overline{}$$
$$\$26{,}250 \text{ profit}$$

"Now *that's* more like it," said Barnabas Brambles, his lips curling to form a greedy grin.

Next, he wrote a to-do list. It was short.

TO DO

1) Make $$$ for me.

Then Barnabas Brambles called a meeting. When all the performers had gathered, he made an announcement.

"There's one word for this circus," he said. "Do you know what that word is?"

"TERRIBLE!" Barnabas Brambles

said in a terribly loud voice.

"Oh my goodness," murmured Elsa. The elderly elephant did not like loud noises.

"You have been pampered and spoiled for years," Barnabas Brambles continued. "Someone needs to crack the whip around here. That someone is me!"

SNAP!
CRACK!
WHaaaaP!

"Hey, watch it!" said Leo. "You could hurt someone with that whip."

"I certainly *could* hurt someone," Barnabas Brambles threatened. "Now listen up. I'm making some changes around here, beginning with your diets. From now on, you'll get one meal a day. This will trim both your bellies and my budget. It's called *downsizing.*"

"Sir Sidney won't like this," said Stan Banana. He was the top Banana because he was older than his twin brother by one minute.

"Sir Sidney won't like this one bit," agreed Dan Banana, the younger brother and second Banana.

WHAAAAP!

"**DON'T** mention Sir Sidney's name again," Barnabas Brambles ordered. "**I'M** the boss now, and **I** make the rules."

Gert, a friendly little mouse, looked up at Barnabas Brambles from the entrance to the tiny mouse hole she shared with Bert, her brother.

"I'd like to tailor that man's suit," Gert whispered to Bert. "Look how poorly it fits him in the shoulders."

"Where?" asked Bert.

Gert scampered up Barnabas Brambles's body. "See?" she said. "Right here."

"*Ack!*" Barnabas Brambles shrieked. "What was that? It looked like a m-m-m-mouse!"

Gert slid down his back.

Bert laughed. "Ha! How do you like that? A lion tamer who's afraid of mice."

Leo cleared his throat. "Mr. Brambles, we have two small friends named Gert and Bert. These mice have traveled with the circus for years."

"They're quite helpful," Elsa added. "Gert and Bert clean up the spilled popcorn after every show with the help of Old Coal, our resident crow."

"Two mice? A *crow*?" said Barnabas Brambles with alarm. "Oh no, no, no. There will be no vermin in my circus."

His circus?

What's *vermin*?

Vermin are animals—including mammals, birds, and insects—that are destructive or annoying. Mice, rats, crows, and cockroaches are all examples of vermin.

"Luckily," Barnabas Brambles said, "I know how to get rid of annoying creatures."

He added a second task to his to-do list.

TO DO
1) Make $$$ for me.
2) Get rid of two mice and one crow.

"Now pay attention," Barnabas Brambles said. "Tomorrow we'll be in Peoria, Illinois, for three shows."

"*Three* shows in one day?" said Leo. "But that's impossible."

"But Elsa has been with Sir Sidney's Circus for years," said Leo. "You can't get rid of her."

"Oh, *can't* I?" Barnabas Brambles sneered. "I can replace anyone I want, including you."

"Out with the old, in with the new! That's my motto," Barnabas Brambles stated.

"You're going to *sell* Elsa and Leo?" Stan Banana asked.

"When?" added Dan Banana.

"When the time is right," said Barnabas Brambles. "I expect big things to happen in Las Vegas."

"Las Vegas?" said Gert, shaking her tiny head. "This is all very dramastic."

"*Dramastic?*" said Bert. "That's not a word, Gert."

"It should be. Dramatic plus drastic. *Dramastic!*"

dramatic + drastic = dramastic

"Are you making up words again?" Bert asked.

Gert smiled. "*Nes.* That's no plus yes."

no + yes = nes

"But where will Leo and I go?" Elsa wondered aloud.

"What will we do?" Leo asked.

"You'll retire, just like Sir Sidney," Barnabas Brambles explained. "I will put you out to pasture. Or if you prefer, you could spend your final days in a smelly zoo."

"Will Leo and I be together?" Elsa asked. She was trying not to cry, but just the thought of leaving Sir Sidney's Circus made her sniffle a little.

"I'm sure I could find a place for both of you," Barnabas Brambles said. "In fact . . . "

The wheels began turning in Barnabas Brambles's darkened brain. He secretly added a third item to his evil to-do list.

TO DO
1) Make $$$ for me.
2) Get rid of two mice and one crow.
3) Sell elephant and lion to zoo for lots of $$$.

"Well, then," Barnabas Brambles said, rubbing his meaty hands together. "I think that's enough chitchat for one meeting. Rest up and get ready for tomorrow's performances. Oh, and Famous Flying Banana Brothers?"

"Yes?" Stan and Dan Banana answered at the same time.

"Learn how this train operates. From now on, you'll be our conductor, Dan, and our navigator, Stan. Our first stop is Peoria."

Any Birdbrain Can Conduct a Train

Barnabas Brambles threw them a book.

"Buckle your seat belt," Bert whispered. "It's going to be a bumpy ride."

That night the animals gathered in the sleeping car for their own meeting. The mood was grim.

"What was Sir Sidney *thinking*?" Leo asked. "How could he have trusted his circus to a horrible man like Barnabas Brambles?"

"I must write to my cousin Louise in London," Elsa said. "Maybe she can tell us something about Barnabas Brambles."

From the Desk of Elsa

Chicago, Illinois

September 1

96 Euston Road

London NW1 2DB

United Kingdom

Dear Cousin Louise,

Have you ever heard of a man named Barnabas Brambles? He claims to be a graduate of the University of Piccadilly Circus.

If you have any information about this man, please write back. I'll be in San Francisco by the end of the week.

Kisses and peanuts to you,

xo *Cousin Elsa*

Elsa gave the letter to Old Coal to deliver.

Never trust a lion tamer in a poorly tailored suit. That's my motto.

I thought you were going to tailor his suit for him.

I am. Come on.

And the two mice scurried off to find the new circus manager.

Meanwhile, in another car of the train, Barnabas Brambles was printing posters and tickets for the upcoming shows.

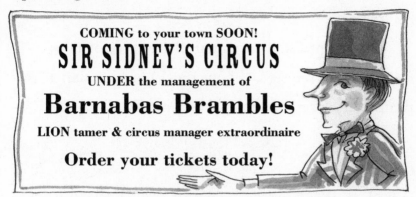

COMING to your town SOON!
SIR SIDNEY'S CIRCUS
UNDER the management of
Barnabas Brambles
LION tamer & circus manager extraordinaire
Order your tickets today!

Meanwhile, in the engine of the train, the Famous Flying Banana Brothers were trying to learn how to read a map.

"But we already know the four directions," Stan Banana said. "Up, down, this way, that way."

"That's what I thought," said Dan Banana. "But look what it says here."

Meanwhile, on his private peanut farm in Georgia, Sir Sidney was trying to enjoy the peace and quiet of country life. But gazing at the moon only made him miss his friends.

"They've probably forgotten all about me by now," he said with a sad sigh. "I hope they're making Barnabas Brambles feel right at home. He's one of a kind."

One of a kind, indeed. If Sir Sidney only knew . . .

CHAPTER TWO

The next day was **Monday**.

The Famous Flying Banana Brothers were up early, studying the map.

"Peoria is w-a-a-ay over here, see?" said Stan Banana. "We'll never get there in time to do three shows."

"We better take a shortcut," said Dan Banana.

So the Famous Flying Banana Brothers derailed the train from the track and took a more, well, *acrobatic* route.

First, they performed a graceful leap over the Missouri River.

Then they pirouetted across the plains of Kansas.

Next, they bravely backflipped the train across the
Colorado Rockies.

Then they catapulted over the Grand Canyon.

Two hours later, they were in Peoria . . . Arizona.

"What? Where? How?" babbled Barnabas Brambles.

"On-time delivery, boss," said Stan Banana.

"But where are all the people?" asked Dan Banana. "Where are our fans?"

"In Peoria, ILLINOIS!" Barnabas Brambles barked. "That's exactly **ONE THOUSAND SIX HUNDRED AND THIRTY MILES FROM HERE!**"

"Oh," said Stan Banana quietly.

"Who knew?" added Dan Banana.

"**EVERYBODY** knows that except you two bozos!" Barnabas Brambles said through gritted teeth. His breath smelled vaguely of grilled onions and spoiled milk.

"There shouldn't be two cities with the same name," said Stan Banana.

"There shouldn't be two brothers with half a **BRAIN** between them!" shouted Barnabas Brambles.

But Barnabas Brambles wasn't listening to the mice. He took his schedule from his pocket. With one stroke of his pen, he canceled the first day's performances.

This Week's Performances

~~Peoria (Monday)~~
ST. LOUIS (TUESDAY)
Tulsa (Wednesday)
OKLAHOMA CITY (THURSDAY)
Denver (Friday)
LAS VEGAS (SATURDAY)
San Francisco (Sunday)

"Can you get this train to St. Louis by tomorrow?" he asked the Famous Flying Banana Brothers.

"St. Louis?" Stan Banana said. "Is that in . . . Louisiana?"

"Missouri!" Barnabas Brambles brayed. "St. Louis is in Missouri!"

"We can do it, boss," Dan Banana said. "No worries."

And so, while the Famous Flying Banana Brothers attempted to get the circus train back on track, Barnabas Brambles studied his to-do list.

"I won't make any money today," he grumbled. "But at least I can get rid of two mice. Let's see. I know I have a book around here somewhere. Oh, here it is."

Any Louse Can Catch a Mouse

He opened the book to the first page.

CHAPTER ONE

So you want to catch a mouse, eh? No worries! Any louse can do it.

Just set a trap with bait. The best mouse baits are:

- cheese
- blueberry pancakes
- peanut butter

"Aha!" Barnabas Brambles said as he pulled a jar of peanut butter from his briefcase. He opened the jar and carefully set two mousetraps. "That'll take care of those little beasts."

Gert and Bert heard every word.

"He must have a low opinion of us if he thinks we'd be tempted by *that* stuff," Bert said with a sniff. "I refuse to eat any peanut butter other than Sir Sidney's special gourmet blend."

"Pay no attention," Gert replied. "I'm almost finished tailoring his suit. There!" She draped the jacket over the back of a chair just in time.

"Where is my jacket?" Barnabas Brambles asked. "Oh, here it is."

The jacket was now three sizes too big.

"Good heavens," whispered Gert. "Look what I've done!"

"Have I lost weight?" Barnabas Brambles said, gazing in the mirror.

"He looks like a clown," Bert said with a giggle. "That's fitting, don't you think?"

"No, no, no," said Gert, who was always more serious than her brother. "It's worse than before. I'll have to try again later."

At six o'clock that night, the circus performers were sitting down to their only meal of the day: goulash.

Goopy Goulash

10 cups blah
8 cups blech
½ gallon pond scum
Dash of icky powder

Mix ingredients halfheartedly. Serve lukewarm. Stale bread optional.

Barnabas Brambles dished up the goopy goulash. "You don't need more than one meal a day," he said. "Not when the food is this delicious and nutritious."

Everyone felt as miserable as mud.

"I'm still hungry," Elsa said when she'd finished.

"Me, too," Leo agreed.

Elsa sighed. "I miss Sir Sidney's peanuts."

"I miss Sir Sidney," Leo added.

And of course, Sir Sidney missed his friends. He even dreamed about them that night at his private peanut farm.

Barnabas Brambles dreamed only of money.

And Elsa? She dreamed about peanuts.

Elsa's dream was so vivid, she could even *smell* peanuts.
In the middle of the night, she began sleepwalking.

"YEEEOOOOW!" Elsa screamed.
"OOOOWWW! AYYYYYYY!"

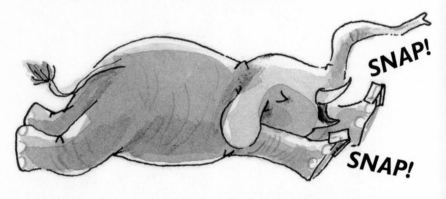

SNAP!

SNAP!

Leo rushed to Elsa's side. "What happened?"

"Mousetraps!" Elsa cried through her tears.

"Oh, let me help," Leo said. "Does it hurt terribly?"
He soothed Elsa as he removed the traps from her feet as
gently as possible.

"It hurts a lot," said Elsa.

Bert and Gert darted out of the mouse hole when they heard the ruckus.

"Oh no!" said Bert. "We saw Barnabas Brambles set those terrible traps. We should have warned everyone."

"You poor dear," Gert said. "Here, let me wrap your sore feet."

They all watched as Gert ran in circles around Elsa's left foot with a long bandage.

"You'll have to take time off," Leo told Elsa. "You're in no condition to perform."

"I suppose you're right," Elsa replied. She was trying not to cry, but it wasn't easy.

"You must rest," Gert said. "It's the only way to get better."

An hour later, Elsa returned to bed with the help of her friends. The rocking motion of the train helped her fall asleep.

But she was still hungry. Everyone was. And it wasn't just food they were hungry for. They were hungry for something better.

That something was actually *someone*—Sir Sidney.

CHAPTER THREE

On **Tuesday** morning, the circus train was gliding gracefully across the Missouri prairie.

"We're still a long way from St. Louis," Stan Banana said, studying the map.

"Mr. Brambles will be mad if we're late," Dan Banana added. "What should we do?"

"What we do best," Stan Banana concluded.

So in the interest of time, the Famous Flying Banana Brothers performed a giant loop-the-loop across the state of Missouri.

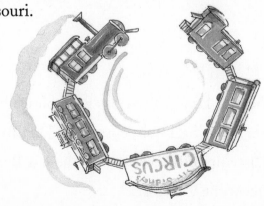

The train landed on top of the St. Louis Arch.

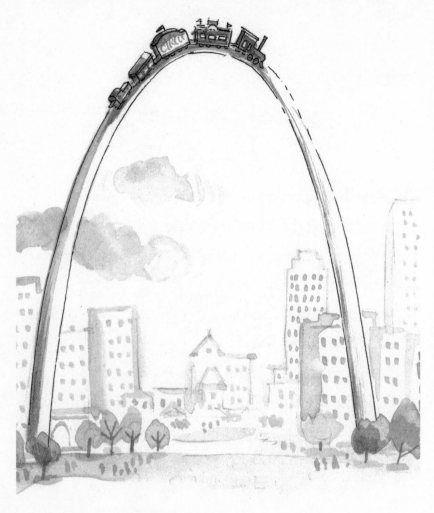

"Bulls-eye!" cried Stan Banana.

"What? Where? How?" Barnabas Brambles babbled.

"Pretty sure this is St. Louis, boss," said Dan Banana. "That's the Mississippi River. And over there is Busch Stadium, home of the Cardinals."

"And this must be the famous Gateway Arch," Stan Banana said.

"I *KNOW* this is the Arch, you worthless rubber-band-for-brains!" Barnabas Brambles bellowed.

"The question is, what are we doing on **TOP** of it?"

"Ever hear of making a grand entrance?" Dan Banana asked with a shrug.

"A grand *entrance*?" yelled Barnabas Brambles. "Where's the *exit*?"

The wind was picking up and the train was starting to sway in the breeze.

"I have to find someone with a crane," Barnabas Brambles declared. Just then he spotted a sign for "Hank's Crane Service." He looked up the number and dialed it.

Barnabas Brambles pulled out the schedule and his pen. He made the necessary changes.

This Week's Performances

CANCELED ~~Peoria (Monday)~~
~~ST. LOUIS (TUESDAY)~~
~~Tulsa (Wednesday)~~
~~OKLAHOMA CITY (THURSDAY)~~
Denver (Friday)
LAS VEGAS (SATURDAY)
San Francisco (Sunday)

"I haven't made any money yet," he said. "Not even a thin dime. And if those empty traps are any indication, I haven't caught any mice yet, either. *Drrrrr.*"

But Barnabas Brambles had an idea. He pulled a piece of mushroom pizza from his pocket. It was two weeks old.

certified organic mold spores

He laughed. "Ha! If there are any hungry mice on this train, let them eat moldy mushroom pizza. That will give 'em a bellyache."

I'd like to give that guy a knuckle sandwich.

But can you *smell* that pizza? It's attracting flies!

Bert, please. No rough talk. It's unattractive.

Barnabas Brambles put the pizza on a pretty plate. Then he placed the plate on the floor of the dining car.

"Aw! Aw!" said Old Coal. The black crow had just returned from London. She flew through the open window to sniff the pizza.

"Ugh!" said Barnabas Brambles with disgust. "I forgot about that wretched crow. How can I get rid of it? Oh, wait. I have an idea!"

He stuffed his jacket with unsold circus tickets and hung it on a coat rack, along with his hat. He set the figure on top of the train. "There!" he said. "A *scarecrow*!"

Barnabas Brambles reviewed his to-do list.

> ## TO DO
> 1) Make $$$ for me.
> 2) Get rid of two mice and one crow.
> 3) Sell elephant and lion to zoo for
>   lots of $$$.

"Hmmm, if I remember correctly, St. Louis has a first-class zoo," he said. "I wonder if the zookeeper is in a buying mood."

As he explained his location, Barnabas Brambles used a second phone to text Cool Cats R Us.

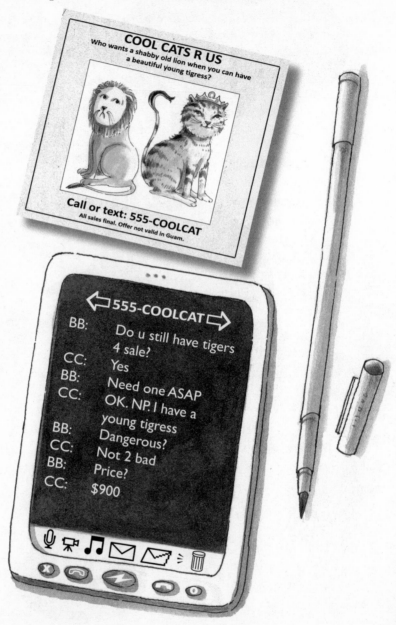

COOL CATS R US
Who wants a shabby old lion when you can have a beautiful young tigress?

Call or text: 555-COOLCAT
All sales final. Offer not valid in Guam.

←555-COOLCAT→

BB: Do u still have tigers 4 sale?
CC: Yes
BB: Need one ASAP
CC: OK. NP. I have a young tigress
BB: Dangerous?
CC: Not 2 bad
BB: Price?
CC: $900

Barnabas Brambles did the math. If he sold Leo for one thousand dollars and bought the new tiger for nine hundred dollars, he would make one hundred dollars. It was nothing to write home about, but it was one hundred dollars more than he had made in ticket sales.

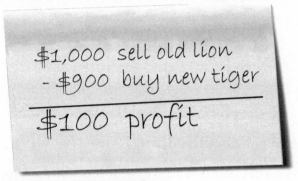

$1,000 sell old lion
-$900 buy new tiger

$100 profit

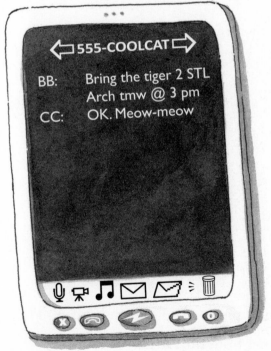

555-COOLCAT

BB: Bring the tiger 2 STL
Arch tmw @ 3 pm

CC: OK. Meow-meow

He wrote one last text message.

Barnabas Brambles was so excited at the thought of making one hundred dollars, he forgot to worry about being stuck on top of the St. Louis Arch. He forgot to care about canceling several shows.

"One hundred dollars!" he said, doing a little dance. "Why, I could buy a fancy hat or a new whip or lots of candy or . . ."

He was so excited at the thought of one hundred dollars, he even forgot to give the circus performers their one measly meal of the day.

Elsa didn't mind. She was still recovering from her mousetrap injuries.

The Famous Flying Banana Brothers didn't care. They were too busy swinging from the Arch.

Gert and Bert were up to their little mouse eyeballs in a sewing project.

"Why do you want to tailor a jacket for that scoundrel?" Bert asked.

"Because," Gert replied firmly, "if the man had clothes that fit him better, he might see fit to be a better man. It's worth a try, anyway."

Old Coal caught her own dinner in the mighty Mississippi River.

Aw!
Aw!

Leo's belly growled as he watched the crow catch fish. The poor lion was famished.

Very late on Tuesday night, Leo sneaked into the dining car.

"Oh, so Mr. Brambles *did* remember to feed us after all," Leo said, spying the moldy mushroom pizza. "I know I should share this with the others, but I'm so hungry. And I love pizza so much."

Bit by bit, Leo ate every bite of the moldy mushroom pizza.

Mmmmmm Mmmmmm Mmmmm Yum yum yum

Then he licked the plate.

SSSHHHHLLLLURP!

Then he rubbed his tummy.

"Ugh," he said a minute later. "Maybe I ate too much." He staggered across the dining car. "*Blegh*. I feel a little—*BLURP!*"

"Excuse *you!*" said Gert, sticking her head out of the mouse hole.

"Sorry," said Leo. "It's just that I—"

BLUUUURRRRRRRRRRRRRRP

"Good heavens!" Gert said. "What's gotten into you, Leo?"

"I don't know," said the lion. "I just had a little snack and—"

BLUUUUUUUUUHHHRRRRPTH

"Leo!" said Gert with alarm. "You are turning the most putrid shade of green. What did you eat? Tell me."

"I ate the snack Mr. Brambles left out for us," Leo replied. "I'm sorry I didn't offer to share it with you, but it was pizza. And I can't resist pizza."

"Bert!" Gert shouted into the mouse hole. "Come quickly! Leo ate the moldy mushroom pizza. I'm afraid he might have food poisoning!"

Gert and Bert quickly built a pump to remove the toxic pizza from Leo's stomach.

The pumping process wasn't pretty. The sounds weren't pretty, either.

BLUURP!   BLOOOP!   BLECHPTZ!

The smells were downright ugly.

PLLLLOOFFT!   FLLLARTZZ!

"There's no need to apologize," Gert said. "Are you feeling better?"

"Yes," Leo said, sniffling softly. "You saved my life."

"You're still very weak," Gert observed. "And a bit green, too."

"Good thing we don't have to perform tomorrow," said Elsa, who had joined the others. "Neither of us is in show shape now."

"You must rest," Gert ordered. "Both of you."

"Leo looks terrible," Bert said.

"*Shhh,*" whispered Gert. "No one likes to hear that."

That is true, of course. No one likes to be told he or she looks terrible, just as no one likes to be sick alone.

"Remember last year when we all had the flu?" Gert asked, trying to change the subject. "Sir Sidney made cinnamon toast and tea for us, and he scratched our backs and rubbed our foreheads. Wasn't that nice?"

"Yes," whispered Elsa. "That was very nice."

"It was," agreed Leo.

No one spoke for a minute as they all recalled the happy memory.

"I miss Sir Sidney," Leo said softly. "He's always so kind to us. He would never give anyone moldy mushroom pizza." Leo began to cry again.

"I know," said Gert softly. "I know."

When it was clear they would all be sleeping together, Gert crawled on top of Leo's belly. The heat of her small body was like a tiny hot water bottle on Leo's sore tummy.

It wasn't as good as Sir Sidney's back scratches, but it was nice. And sometimes nice is enough to get you through a bad night.

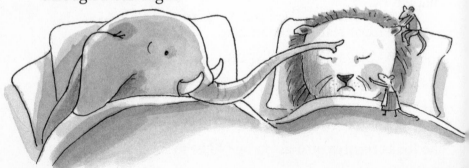

❧CHAPTER FOUR❧

By **Wednesday** morning, little had changed. The train was still dangling dangerously from the St. Louis Arch.

Elsa's feet were still sore.

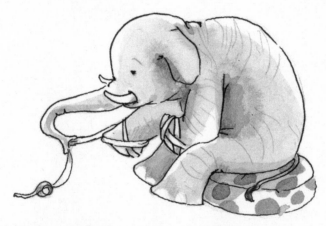

And Leo was still as weak as a kitten.

But Barnabas Brambles was in a banner mood. "Good morning," he said brightly. "Today is a big day!"

He pulled on his jacket, which Gert had just finished altering. It now looked twelve sizes too small.

"It's not funny," said Gert. "The man needs a jacket that fits him properly. Maybe I should make him a brand-new suit. Yes, that's what I'll do!"

Barnabas Brambles didn't hear the mice talking. He had other matters on his mind.

"We have important business to conduct today," he said. "I've rigged up a simple elevator. I'm going to send Leo down on it. When the new tiger is delivered, I'll use the elevator to bring her up. Watch this!"

He demonstrated the new device.

"Just looking at that elevator makes me queasy," Leo said from the train window.

"*Queasy?*" said Barnabas Brambles. "Why?"

"Because I ate a piece of moldy mushroom pizza last night," Leo answered. "My tummy still feels funny."

"Tough luck," said Barnabas Brambles. "That's what you get for stealing food. The moldy mushroom pizza was not intended for you. It was mouse bait."

"I wish you wouldn't try to hurt our small friends," Leo said bravely. "Or us."

"Chin up, old chap," Barnabas Brambles said with a wave of his hand. "Your pizza predicament will be a good story to tell your new friends in the zoo."

"New *friends*?" Elsa asked, suddenly concerned.

"Zoo?" added Leo.

"That's right," Barnabas Brambles said. "I'm selling—er, *sending*—you to the zoo. You'll love it there. I hear the cages are very comfortable."

"If Leo goes, I go, too," said Elsa. "We're best friends."

"Sorry," said Barnabas Brambles. "The zoo doesn't need an elephant. Just a lion."

"But you said we could go together," Elsa reminded him.

"I lied," Barnabas Brambles replied with a wicked grin.

HONK
HONK!
HONK!
Honk!

Just then the zookeeper arrived. She was driving a snazzy zoomobile. It had an unusual horn.

"Anybody up there?" the zookeeper hollered.

"Yes, we're here!" Barnabas Brambles yelled, waving his arms. "I'll have your classic cat ready in a jiffy!" He turned to Leo. "Get in the box."

"But I don't want to get in that box," Leo replied. "And I don't want to go to the zoo if Elsa's not going."

"I said, GET IN THE BOX. **NOW!**"

"And *I* said I don't want to get in that box. I don't want to go—"

Barnabas Brambles reached for his whip.

No one had ever cracked a whip at Leo—certainly not Sir Sidney. He never even raised his voice.

A trembling Leo crawled into the box.

Barnabas Brambles nailed the lid shut. "There. That's better."

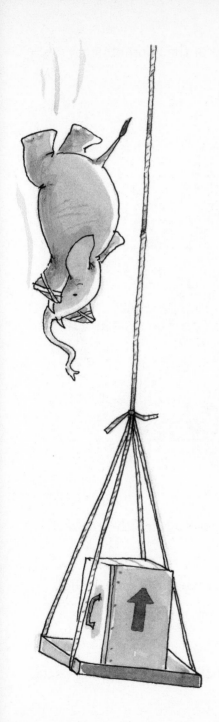

"Where's my lion?" the zookeeper yelled through cupped hands.

"Coming right up—er, I mean *down*!" Barnabas Brambles hollered back. Slowly, he lowered the elevator as everyone watched nervously.

"Let's take this easy . . . easy . . . easy . . . ," Barnabas Brambles said.

It was too much for Elsa. "If Leo's leaving the circus," she announced, "then I'm going with him."

And with that, Elsa performed an elegant swan dive from the top of the Arch.

She landed squarely on top of the zoomobile.

BLAM!

"Your elephant ruined my zoomobile!" the zookeeper shouted.

"Send me the bill later," Barnabas Brambles yelled back. "Right now you can pay me for the cat. One thousand smackeroos, please."

"I must inspect the feline before I pay anything," said the zookeeper.

The zookeeper put on her special inspection spectacles. Then she pried open the box. Leo practically poured out.

"I don't need to see or *smell* any more of this," said the zookeeper, holding her nose and removing her glasses.

"I'm waiting for my money," Barnabas Brambles barked from the top of the Arch.

"Aren't you listening?" cried the zookeeper. "I don't *want* this cat! He's not well. He'll make my other animals sick."

"Oh, Leo's not contagious," Barnabas Brambles said casually. "He just ate a little moldy mushroom pizza."

"*Moldy mushroom pizza?*" cried the zookeeper. "That can cause witzelsucht!"

Witzelsucht is the excessive and inappropriate use of silly or pointless humor. The word comes from the German words *witzeln,* meaning "to joke," and *sucht,* meaning "habit."

Bert, is that what you have?

Witzelsucht? Sure, I'll try it. Make mine with sauerkraut.

"Good-bye, Mr. Brambles," said the zookeeper firmly. "I am returning your sick cat along with your elephant. I will send you the bill for my zoomobile."

Leo and Elsa rode the homemade elevator to the top of the Arch.

"Drrrrr," Barnabas Brambles growled as he unloaded the cargo.

A few minutes later, a second vehicle arrived. It was a sleek sports car painted in a tiger-print pattern. A fancy lady climbed out. She was wearing a tiger-print pantsuit.

I'm looking for someone named BB who ordered a tiger!

"Huh?" said Barnabas Brambles. In all the commotion, he had forgotten about the tiger.

"I'm here to deliver a tiger," the lady said.

"Oh yeah," Barnabas Brambles hollered down. "Send her up. I must inspect the feline before I pay anything." (Barnabas Brambles had learned a thing or two from the zookeeper.)

"Sorry," the lady replied. "You have to pay first. If not, I'll sell this prized tigress to someone else. Do you want her or don't you?"

"Oh, all right," Barnabas Brambles grumbled.

"Nine hundred dollars," said the lady. "Please."

Barnabas Brambles wrote a check and sent it down in the elevator.

Everyone watched as the elevator rose slowly in the
sunlight.

Barnabas Brambles grabbed his whip. He didn't mind putting others in danger, but he rarely put himself in harm's way.

"Now listen here, you," he said, speaking directly to the box. "I am opening this box. And when I do, I want you to know that I am the boss. I am a professional lion tamer. I am also certified to train tigers, cougars, and panthers. So don't try anything fancy with me."

"He's stalling," observed Gert.

"For a lion tamer, he's a bit of a scaredy cat," said Bert.

Barnabas Brambles was still speaking to the unopened box. "I know you're a tiger, so you probably think you're hot stuff. But when I open this box, don't even *think* about trying anything funny with me. Because I assure you that if you do, there will be trouble, BIG trouble, because I am a professional lion—"

Just then the box popped open. Out crawled a . . .

"Her name is Tiger," the lady in the pantsuit yelled back.

"But she's a *kitten*!"

"With tiger stripes," added the lady. "Good-bye."

"Stop!" screamed Barnabas Brambles. "I want my money back!"

"Sor-r-r-ry," sang the lady from her sports car. "All sales are final. *Meow-meow.*"

The animals gathered around the kitten.

Aw! Aw!

Welcome to Sir Sidney's Circus.

You'll like Sir Sidney a whole lot better than this Brambles guy.

We hope you'll be happy here.

May we call you Tiger?

Mrrrare. Mrrare.

"*Drrrrr*," said Barnabas Brambles. "This has been a big day, all right—a big *bad* day."

❧ CHAPTER FIVE ❧

On **Thursday** Barnabas Brambles waited for the crane operator to come and remove the train from the top of the St. Louis Arch.

He waited.

And waited.   And waited.

Finally, at six o'clock in the evening, he called the crane operator.

Barnabas Brambles took out his show schedule. With a black pen he drew lines through FRIDAY and SATURDAY.

This Week's Performances

CANCELED ~~Peoria (Monday)~~
~~ST. LOUIS (TUESDAY)~~
~~Tulsa (Wednesday)~~
~~OKLAHOMA CITY (THURSDAY)~~
~~Denver (Friday)~~
~~LAS VEGAS (SATURDAY)~~
San Francisco (Sunday)

"Only one day left," Barnabas Brambles said to himself.

"And something tells me it's going to be a doozy," said Bert.

CHAPTER SIX

Friday was a long day. The train was still stuck. Elsa and Leo were still recovering from their injuries. And Barnabas Brambles was still wearing a suit that looked twelve sizes too small.

"The problem," said Gert, "is that I'm not big enough to properly measure him." She was standing in front of Barnabas Brambles's feet.

"I'm not much help in that department," Bert said.

Just then Old Coal arrived at the window. "Aw! Aw!" the black crow cried.

"Hello, Old Coal," said Gert. "Would you do me a favor? Put this tape measure in your beak and fly around Mr. Brambles."

Old Coal did as requested.

"Thank you," said Gert. "Now that I have his accurate measurements, I can sew Mr. Brambles a new suit."

Barnabas Brambles didn't notice Gert or Bert, but he did see Old Coal. "Ack!" he said. "There's that awful crow again. Why isn't my scarecrow working?"

In fact, the scarecrow *was* working, but not in the way Barnabas Brambles had planned. It was attracting vultures. The bald birds were circling overhead.

"They must think that scarecrow is their next meal," Barnabas Brambles said.

As the day wore on, the vultures became bolder. Barnabas Brambles tried to scare them away with his whip.

But the vultures remained. The sight of Barnabas Brambles waving his whip attracted even *more* vultures.

"This is getting scary," said Elsa as day turned into night. She and Leo were watching from the dining car window.

"I'm right here, pal," Leo assured Elsa.

Barnabas Brambles waved his whip until his arms wore out. When he finally gave up, Old Coal flew by with what looked like a smile on her beak.

"I know," said Bert. "But she's still lucky. Boy, I wish I could fly. Wouldn't that be sweet? Too bad we don't have wings."

"The Famous Flying Banana Brothers don't have wings, and *they* know how to fly," said Gert.

"I never thought of that," said Bert. "I should ask the Banana brothers to teach me to fly on a trapeze. Great idea, Gert. Thanks!"

Gert's little brain was so focused on her sewing, a full minute passed before she realized what Bert had said.

"He's going to learn how to *fly*?" she said to herself. "Oh dear."

CHAPTER SEVEN

On **Saturday** the crane operator
arrived with a large Siberian crane.

Using his strong jaw, the crane lifted the train off the Arch.

"Finally!" said Barnabas Brambles when the train was back on solid ground.

The crane operator handed Barnabas Brambles a bill.

HANK'S CRANE SERVICE

For services rendered: $2,000

Payment terms: Give me the money now. Or else.

Two thousand dollars? That's not fair!

Fair is fowl and fowl is fair.

The crane operator studied the check. "I've never heard of First Bank of Lion Tamers. Where is it?"

"Here," said Barnabas Brambles. And he threw the crane operator a book.

Later that evening as the train rolled along the rails, Old Coal arrived with a letter.

"What's this?" Barnabas Brambles snarled.

He opened the letter and read it.

SIR SIDNEY'S CIRCUS

Sir Sidney
Owner and Founder

September 7

Dear Mr. Brambles,

I am writing from my private peanut farm to let you know I will be at tomorrow night's show in San Francisco. Please tell Elsa that I will bring her plenty of fresh peanuts from my farm. Also, will you kindly tell Leo I have some new hairbrushes for him?

I must tell you, Mr. Brambles, that I knew being away from my friends for a whole week would be difficult. But I had no idea just how *much* I'd miss them. Thank you for taking good care of everyone. It means the world to me.

I'll see you tomorrow night at seven o'clock.

Sincerely,

Sir Sidney

Sir Sidney

P.S. Please give Old Coal a generous serving of sunflower seeds. She's made a very long journey today and deserves a good dinner.

But Barnabas Brambles didn't give the tired crow a good dinner. He didn't give *anyone* a dinner, good or otherwise. He was too busy worrying about Sir Sidney's return. "To–to–tomorrow night?" he mumbled nervously. "Sir Sidney will be back to–to–tomorrow night?"

⚘ CHAPTER EIGHT ⚘

A full moon hung in the sky as Sir Sidney's circus train somersaulted its way across the country.

But by **Sunday** afternoon, the train had made it only as far as Las Vegas, hundreds of miles from San Francisco.

"Can't you make this thing go any faster?" Barnabas Brambles asked.

"You want to go *faster*?" Stan Banana replied.

"Yes!" snapped Barnabas Brambles. "We missed the morning show and the three o'clock show, too. In order to make the seven o'clock show, we *must* go faster."

And with that, the Famous Flying Banana Brothers took a deep breath. Then they performed the most spectacular trick ever seen in Las Vegas—maybe in the whole world.

They blasted the circus train in the air, turning two and a half revolutions.

Then they jackknifed the train into a swimming pool.

When the train resurfaced, it gleamed and glistened like a new toy.

Then it shot like an arrow through the sky, down into California, and across the state to the San Francisco Bay, where it landed with a gentle *ploop* on the Golden Gate Bridge.

The vultures, who had been following the train from Missouri, circled overhead.

"Tell me this isn't happening," Barnabas Brambles said in a tired voice. "This can't be happening."

But it was true.

The train was stuck again in a most stupendous style.

"We'll never make it to the seven o'clock show," said Barnabas Brambles sadly.

"Wait!" said Stan Banana. "Everyone lean this way."

Everyone leaned to the right. The train moved slightly right.

"Now everyone lean this way," said Dan Banana.

They did, and the train moved slightly left.

"Now everyone jump up and down," said Stan Banana.

Everyone jumped up and down.

"Now everyone do the hokeypokey," said Dan Banana.

Everyone did the hokeypokey. Er, *almost* everyone.

"Don't be ridiculous!" cried Barnabas Brambles. "This will never work!"

But just then, the train started to move.

Slowly, like a stream of thick maple syrup poured from a pitcher, the train slid from the top of the bridge to the bottom.

"Well done, boys!" said Gert.

"Thanks!" said Stan Banana with pride.

"Where to, boss?" Dan Banana asked.

The train flew faster than the wind across the city to the circus grounds, where a huge crowd was waiting.

"Hurry!" said Barnabas Brambles. "The show begins in one hour! Everybody get ready."

"But I'm still sick," said Leo. "I can't do tricks with a sick belly."

"And I can't dance with these bandages on my feet," said Elsa.

"Ack!" said Barnabas Brambles. "Oh, I suppose you're right. That means the Famous Flying Banana Brothers will have to carry the entire show. Where are those Bananas?"

"Sleeping," said Leo.

"They take a nap after every performance," Elsa explained. "Their tricks today were quite impressive. They'll probably sleep for hours."

"But look at all the *people* who have come to tonight's show!" Barnabas Brambles said, his voice rising. "I've sold a thousand tickets! Don't you understand? You *have* to perform. Sir Sidney will be in the audience!"

"Oh, he wouldn't want to see me performing in this condition," Leo said.

"Or me like this," Elsa said.

Barnabas Brambles put his head in his hands. He knew Leo and Elsa were right.

He reviewed his to-do list.

> ## TO DO
> 1) Make $$$ for me.
> 2) Get rid of two mice and one crow.
> 3) Sell elephant and lion to zoo for lots of $$$.

Barnabas Brambles had failed at everything he'd set out to do.

As he watched the audience fill the circus tent, he considered his options.

He could run away. It would be easy for him to disappear without having to face Sir Sidney. "I'm tempted to leave this very minute," Barnabas Brambles said to himself.

But he knew the old saying.

The show must go on!

And yet, what kind of show could there possibly be without Elsa, Leo, and the Famous Flying Banana Brothers?

At seven o'clock, Barnabas Brambles slowly walked to the center ring of the circus. The crowd was silent.

You could've heard a popcorn kernel drop.

"Welcome!" Barnabas Brambles said nervously. "We have a, uh, terrific show planned for you tonight. And I'd like to begin by, um, er, uh . . ."

He looked around the circus tent. His gaze stopped on a boy selling popcorn.

"By juggling popcorn balls!" Barnabas Brambles announced. "Young man, give me three of your stickiest popcorn balls!"

The boy did as he was told.

"Stand back," Barnabas Brambles warned. Then, with dramatic flair, he threw the popcorn balls into the air.

The first ball fell to the ground.

PLINK

The second ball flew into the audience.

PLUNK

The third popcorn ball bonked Barnabas Brambles on the head.

PLONK

"Ha ha!" Barnabas Brambles laughed weakly. "Never mind that. Did you know I can turn a cartwheel better than anyone on Earth? Feast your eyes on this!"

He lifted his arms and puffed out his chest. Then he flung his long legs over his hands.

He ripped his pants and landed flat on his back.

The audience began to grumble.

"What kind of lousy show is this?" someone hollered from the back row.

"I paid five dollars for my ticket!" a woman yelled.

"I want a refund!" cried an angry man.

Barnabas Brambles jumped up. "Now hold on here a minute!" he fired back. "Don't blame me. The person you should blame is . . . um, well, er, uh . . ."

He rubbed his chin. He didn't see Bert race up his trousers. The little mouse stood on Barnabas Brambles's shoulder.

Who *should* they blame? Whose fault is this?

"Huh?" Barnabas Brambles said. He was surprised by the question. He thought it was his conscience, that wise little voice in his head he usually ignored.

"I said," Bert whispered loudly, *"whose fault is this?"*

Gert dashed up Barnabas Brambles's other side. "Think about it," she whispered in his right ear.

Barnabas Brambles thought about it.

"Who spent the past week mismanaging the circus?" Bert asked.

"Who was cruel to the animals?" Gert added.

"Who was a scoundrel, a villain, and a vully?" Bert pressed.

"A *vully*," explained Gert, "is my word for a vulgar bully."

"I was," Barnabas Brambles answered sadly.

For the first time in many years, he was being honest. He lifted his head and spoke truthfully to the audience. "Because of my bad choices and terrible behavior, there will be no show this evening. You can all go home."

THAT was the cue.

Bert snapped his fingers. Gert hit the lights. For a few seconds, the audience sat in stunned silence. But when the lights came back on, the real show began. It was a show unlike any other in the world.

(Sing to the tune of "Erie Canal" by Thomas S. Allen)

You came to see a circus show—
Please don't think that you really should go.
We aim to please and not cause woe—
But we think that you really should know:

 We've had a week of ick and gore;
The animals are sick and sore.
But worry not, dear visitor—
Here's a show that you might like more.

 (Chorus)

We're not the ones you came to see.
This show was not supposed to be.
But we hope you like our play.
We hope it makes you say:
"Hey, those Three-Ring Rascals really saved the day!"

Look here and you will see a man—
He adheres to a very mean plan.
But we survived 'cause we're small and wise and—
Thanks to him we now understand:

No matter if you're young or old—
If you're kind, you're good as gold.
And even if you're feeling bold,
Don't eat food if it's covered in mold!

"You're absolutely right!" Barnabas Brambles cried. "I couldn't agree more! Good heavens, I had no idea how clever you tiny vermin are!"

"Would you *stop* calling us vermin already?" said Bert. "We're *mice*. It rhymes with *nice*."

"I see," said Barnabas Brambles. "The rhyme suits you."

"Speaking of suits," whispered Gert. She disappeared for a moment. When she returned, she was pulling the new suit she had made for Barnabas Brambles. "Here, try this on for size."

It fit perfectly.

"I've never had such a nice suit," Barnabas Brambles said. "It fits like a glove. Thank you. What did you say your name was?"

"Gert," the little mouse answered as she extended a tiny paw.

I'm Bert, her brother. And that's Old Coal. We're the ones you were trying to get rid of, remember?

"I do," said Barnabas Brambles. "How awful of me. I don't know what I was thinking. Can you ever forgive me?"

"Of course," said Gert. "Would you like to sing with us?"

"It would be an honor," said Barnabas Brambles, bowing.

Bert snapped his fingers. "Hit me with a hot note, Leo."

(Reprise)

We're not the ones you paid to see.

This show was not supposed to be.

But we hope you like our play.

We hope it makes you say:

"Give the Three-Ring Rascals a big HIP-HIP-HOORAY!"

When they finished, the audience erupted in applause.

YAY!   **Hip hip hooray!**

Cool!   **Wow!**

No one clapped louder than the man sitting in the front row—Sir Sidney.

"There is one word for tonight's performance," he said. "And do you know what that word is?"

"TERRIFIC!"

"Thank you, sir," said Gert. She was grinning from furry ear to furry ear.

"Thanks!" added Bert. "The Famous Flying Banana Brothers taught me some great moves."

"You were both *spectacular*," Sir Sidney said. "And you, Old Coal, are a shy star."

"Aw! Aw!" answered the crow.

"Three-ring rascals, indeed," continued Sir Sidney. "Mr. Brambles, you have breathed new life into my circus. You have given it energy, vision, a new attitude, and vultures. And a tiger-striped kitten! For that I say, bravo. Bravo!"

"Stop, in the name of the law!"

It was the police!

And not just one officer. There were three officers, one police captain, an angry elephant, plus a few familiar faces.

"What's this all about?" asked Sir Sidney.

"Cousin Louise!" cried Elsa. "What are *you* doing here?"

"That man!" Cousin Louise said, pointing with her trunk at Barnabas Brambles. She handed Elsa a poster.

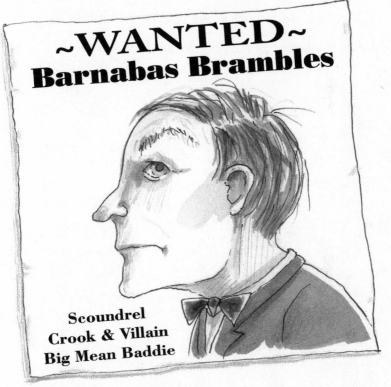

~WANTED~
Barnabas Brambles

**Scoundrel
Crook & Villain
Big Mean Baddie**

"Oh my goodness!" said Elsa, staring at the face she knew too well.

"I called the police as soon as I got your letter," explained Cousin Louise. "Barnabas Brambles is well known in London as the meanest man alive."

"We've had many complaints about Barnabas Brambles in this country, too," said the police captain.

"He ruined my zoomobile," said the zookeeper.

"He gave me a check from a bank that doesn't exist," said the woman in the tiger-striped pantsuit.

"Me, too," added the crane operator. "And he didn't come to my birthday party—or say thank you to my crane."

"He doesn't have a degree in lion taming from the University of Piccadilly Circus," said Cousin Louise. "There's no such school in London—or anywhere. Barnabas Brambles is an expert in one thing only: *lying*."

"Mr. Brambles," said Sir Sidney, turning to face the disgraced manager, "is this true?"

Barnabas Brambles collapsed in a heap. He was exhausted by the disastrous week. And now that his past had caught up with him, he was too ashamed to show his face.

Slowly he stood up and told the truth.

"I deserve it," said Barnabas Brambles sadly. "Sir Sidney, you need to hire a better man."

"Hmm," said Sir Sidney softly. And then he began to pace.

Barnabas Brambles was confused. He thought maybe Sir Sidney hadn't heard him. He peeked through his hands and repeated himself. "I *said* you need to hire a better man."

Sir Sidney stopped pacing. "You're right," he said. "I'd like to hire the man you're going to be tomorrow."

"What?" asked Barnabas Brambles.

"Have you learned anything this week, Mr. Brambles?" Sir Sidney asked.

"Yes," Barnabas Brambles replied.

"Have you gained respect for the members of my circus, both large and small?" Sir Sidney asked.

"I'll say," Barnabas Brambles said, nodding.

"Good," replied Sir Sidney. "Then you'll be a better man tomorrow. And that's the man I'd like to hire."

"I can't believe Sir Sidney is giving him another chance," Elsa said quietly.

"You have to admit, this last week has been entertaining," Leo replied.

"I did drop a few unnecessary pounds," Elsa noted.

"Sir Sidney is a rare man indeed," agreed Leo. "No one treats animals better than Sir Sidney does."

"He's even kind to vermin like Barnabas Brambles," said Bert.

"Ladies and gentlemen!" Sir Sidney said in a loud voice. "I believe the circus has made enough money tonight to reimburse you all for your losses." Then he turned and spoke directly to Barnabas Brambles. "Please pay your debts in full."

Barnabas Brambles added up the ticket sales and subtracted his debts.

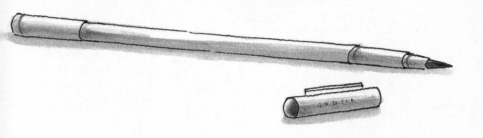

TICKET SALES
1,000 tickets x $5 = $5,000

DEBTS
    London debts $1,000
    Hank's Crane Service $2,000
    Repair of zoomobile $1,099
    Cool Cats R Us $900
                        $4,999

    Ticket sales: $5,000
    Debts: -$4,999
    Profit: $1

"That seems about right," Sir Sidney said with a sly smile. "And don't forget, you owe thousands of children around the country a free show."

"And popcorn," said Bert.

"And lemonade," said Gert.

"Right," said Barnabas Brambles. "Right."

"Now, with the permission of the police," said Sir Sidney, "I'd like Mr. Brambles to remain in my custody. He can work for my circus while he works at becoming a better man."

The police captain thought about this for a moment. "I suppose we could give it a try," she said.

"Good," Sir Sidney said. "Is this okay with you, Cousin Louise?"

"I guess so," she replied. "But the man really is a despicable creature."

"A horrible man," added the zookeeper.

"He didn't even buy me a birthday present," said the crane operator. Then he shrugged and turned to Barnabas Brambles. "Here," he said, taking a piece of cake from his pocket. "I said I'd save you some birthday cake."

After the police left, Barnabas Brambles and Sir Sidney stood in silence for a few minutes. The quiet felt good after all the commotion.

"Why are you giving me a second chance?" asked Barnabas Brambles in a soft voice.

"Because behind every great man is someone who believes in him," said Sir Sidney. "And I don't think anyone has ever believed in you. Am I right?"

"Yes, but how did you know?"

"Oh, I could tell the minute I met you," said Sir Sidney. "The way you bragged. Your lies. Everything about you, in fact."

"But," Sir Sidney continued, "I also knew that underneath it all there was a good man."

"Sir Sidney, *you* are a good man," said Barnabas Brambles. "I want to try to be exactly like you."

"Oh no, don't do that," said Sir Sidney. "Try to be like *you*—the best *you* that you can be. That's the trick."

"Really?" said Barnabas Brambles. "I had no idea."

"It's true," Sir Sidney said.

Barnabas Brambles nodded thoughtfully. "Maybe you're right."

"Sir Sidney is *always* right," whispered Elsa.

"That's why he's Sir Sidney," said Leo.

There's one word for Sir Sidney: *smafunderful.*

smart + fun + wonderful = smafunderful

Did somebody sneeze?

"I'm not a certified lion tamer," said Barnabas Brambles. "But Sir Sidney, you are quite the *liar* tamer."

Sir Sidney chuckled. "Well, I think we've had enough excitement for one day. Let's all go out for a nice meal, shall we? My treat."

"Hooray!" said Bert. "Dinner in a restaurant!"

As they walked to the restaurant, Sir Sidney admired Barnabas Brambles's new clothes.

"That's a very fine suit you're wearing," Sir Sidney said. "May I ask who made it?"

Barnabas Brambles stopped in his tracks when he remembered. "You won't believe it, Sir Sidney, but a *mouse* made this suit for me. Her name's Gert and her brother is Bert, and, well, I think they're simply *remarkable*. In fact, after dinner I'd like to spend some time chatting with those clever mice. They seem to know a *lot* about circus life."

Sir Sidney smiled. Barnabas Brambles was making progress already.

But wait!
There's more!

Here's a sneak peek at

🌿 Three-Ring Rascals, BOOK 2: 🌿

THE GREATEST
STAR ON EARTH

This Way

THE CIRCUS TIMES

"We cover circus news like a tent!"

2002 Bull Street   Savannah, GA 31401

Polly Pumpkinseed
Publisher

October 6

Sir Sidney
c/o Sir Sidney's Circus Train
Somewhere in the USA

Dear Sir Sidney,

Everyone knows your circus is the best circus in the world.
That's good news for you and bad news for me. I'm trying
to sell *newspapers*, Sir Sidney, and you're not giving me
anything *new* to write about!

I have an idea. I'm going to sponsor a contest. The best
performer in your circus will be named the Greatest Star
on Earth. The winner will receive a trophy.

To find out more about this exciting contest, you'll have to
read *The Circus Times*.

Good luck to all and see you soon!

Polly Pumpkinseed

Polly Pumpkinseed

P.S. I know you have many talented performers in your
circus. Unfortunately, I have only *one* trophy.

"Hmm," said Sir Sidney when he'd finished reading the letter. "I'm not sure I like the sound of this contest. I must ponder the situation." He began to pace.

Sir Sidney always paces when he ponders.

He says walking helps him think.

"But look how Sir Sidney is walking," said Elsa.

"He seems so unsteady," said Leo.

Just then Sir Sidney fell.

Oh my gosh!

He fainted!

Thirty minutes later, Dr. Dora Drap arrived.

She measured Sir Sidney's height and weight. She checked his ear wax and tested his belly button.

DING-DONG

Then she listened to his heart.

THUMP THUMP
THUMP THUMP
THUMP THUMP

Finally, Dr. Drap used her special magnifying camera device to take a picture of Sir Sidney's nose. "Aha!" she said. "You have a worrywart, Sir Sidney. See? It's right here." She pointed to a spot on his nose.

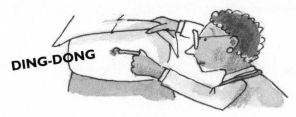

"What are worrywarts caused by?" asked Stan Banana.

"Where do they come from?" added Dan Banana.

Dr. Drap drew a diagram. "Worrywarts can grow anywhere on the body. A patient with a worrywart is usually nervous about something." She turned to look at Sir Sidney. "What's worrying you?"

"Polly Pumpkinseed," said Sir Sidney with a sigh. "She's sponsoring a contest to find the Greatest Star on Earth."

Dr. Drap laughed. "Why worry about that? One of your performers will surely win."

"What should I do?" asked Sir Sidney.

"You should worry less and laugh more," said Dr. Drap. "You also need to rest. I'll write you a prescription."

From the Desk of Dr. Dora Drap

Sir Sidney must rest for one week in a quiet place.

NO worrying!

Sir Sidney studied his instructions. "I could go to my private peanut farm in Georgia and rest there," he said.

Good idea, I'll give you a ride in my plane.

"An airplane ride!" said Leo. "That'll be fun!"

"Sure will," agreed Elsa. "We'll come with you, Sir Sidney."

"No," said Dr. Drap. "Sir Sidney needs peace and quiet."

Sir Sidney turned to his friends. "We must do what the doctor says. Banana brothers, can you drive the train to all the cities on our tour this week?"

"It would be an honor," said Stan Banana.

"A privilege," said Dan Banana.

"Good," said Sir Sidney. "Now, who will be in charge when I'm gone?"

❧ ABOUT THE AUTHOR ❧ AND ILLUSTRATOR

KATE KLISE and **M. SARAH KLISE** are sisters who like to write (Kate) and draw (Sarah). They began making books when they were little girls who shared a bedroom in Peoria, Illinois. Kate now lives and writes in an old farmhouse on forty acres in the Missouri Ozarks. Sarah draws and dwells in a Victorian cottage in Berkeley, California. Together the Klise sisters have created more than twenty award-winning books for young readers. Their goal always is to make the kind of fun-to-read books they loved years ago when they were kids.

To learn more about the Klise sisters, visit their website: www.kateandsarahklise.com.

You might also enjoy visiting Sir Sidney and his friends at www.threeringrascals.com.